Reycraft Books
55 Fifth Avenue
New York, NY 10003

## Reycraftbooks.com

Reycraft Books is a trade imprint and trademark of Newmark Learning, LLC.

This edition is published by arrangement with China Children's Press & Publication Group, China.
© China Children's Press & Publication Group

Educators and Librarians: Our books may be purchased in bulk for promotional, educational, or business use. Please contact sales@reycraftbooks.com.

Library of Congress Control Number: 2020908387

ISBN: 978-1-4788-6978-8

Printed in Dongguan, China. 8557/0720/17254

10 9 8 7 6 5 4 3 2 1

First Edition Hardcover published by Reycraft Books 2020

Reycraft Books and Newmark Learning, LLC, support diversity and the First Amendment, and celebrate the right to read.

**REYCRAFT**
BOOKS

# The Musician

by Xuefeng Liu

illustrated by Gunter Grossholz and Yuxi Wan

In ancient China, a young musician named Yu Boya gained fame for his talents. As a boy, Boya learned to play guqin, a traditional Chinese string instrument. He was so skilled at playing, he was called the "Guqin Sage." Boya liked best of all to play in nature, among animals, rivers, and mountains. When he grew up, he worked as a diplomat. Boya often entertained important officials and nobles with his beautiful music.

Once, Boya went out to the fields to play tunes for the king's horses. The music was so enchanting that the horses forgot to

graze on the delicious grasses.

Boya often traveled to other Chinese states for his work. He always brought an elaborate guqin with him that, according to legend, was created by an ancient Chinese emperor.

One year, Boya set off on a special mission. Just as his boat sailed along the Hanyang River, a violent storm broke. Lightning flashed and sheets of rain poured down. Boya was forced to take shelter on the riverbank, at the foot of a hill.

It just so happened that it was the Moon Festival that day. As evening fell, the wind ceased, and the waves calmed. The clouds dispersed, revealing a brilliant, full moon glowing brightly in the star-studded sky. Boya was so inspired, he pulled out his guqin and began to play.

Captivated by the magnificent scene, Boya played on and on. Suddenly, he noticed a dark figure standing on the riverbank. Scared, his fingers slipped and one of the instrument's strings snapped. The man stepped forward from the shadows. It was a woodcutter.

"I am so sorry to disturb you," he said.

Boya couldn't believe it. *How can a woodcutter understand my music?* he thought. "Please, tell me what song I was playing?"

The woodcutter saluted him and answered, "Sir, you were playing a tune expressing the praise Confucius gave to one of his great disciples. But your string snapped. What a pity!"

When Boya heard this, he was surprised and invited the woodcutter to join him on his boat.

During their conversation, Boya discovered that the woodcutter's name was Zhong Ziqi. He was a scholar living in seclusion. Ziqi was also skilled at playing guqin. He had heard a lot about Boya and was overjoyed to finally meet him. Excited, Boya played his musical masterpiece for him.

When Boya played music in praise of the towering mountains,
Ziqi's eyes brightened.

# "Wonderful!" he cried.

"This melody is as magnificent and dignified as Mount Tai,
whose snowy peak reaches the sky!"

When Boya played music that echoed turbulent waves, Ziqi's eyes widened.

"Wonderful!" he cried.

"This melody is as vast and mighty as the great rivers of China!"

Boya was overcome with excitement. "Only you comprehend all the pictures in my mind. You fully understand my music! I am so grateful to finally have a dear friend like you," he said.

Then he told Ziqi how he learned to play music. Boya also confided in him how he came to create his masterpiece,

## "Lofty Mountains and Flowing Water."

When he was young, Boya learned how to play guqin from his teacher, Chen Lian. He studied for three years. After that, he had a good command of all the skills needed.

His understanding of music, however, was still not deep enough. Boya's playing lacked elegance and passion. When he performed, the audience felt nothing.

One day, Chen Lian said, "I know a teacher who lives on Penglai Island. He could help you improve your playing by stirring your passions." So they took a small boat to the island. But when they arrived, it was empty.

"Stay here and practice playing," Chen Lian told Boya. Then he left to find the teacher.

Boya waited and waited. Several days passed. But Chen Lian never returned. Boya practiced his music, enjoying the stunning scenery that surrounded him.

Every part of nature seemed to have its own song. The running waters gurgled, the flying seagulls squawked, and the green forests whispered their secrets. Together, they composed a beautiful melody.

Boya's mind filled with ideas, and he began to play a new tune on his guqin. He lost track of time as his fingers plucked out a new melody. He realized then why Chen Lian had left him alone on the island. To find inspiration in nature.

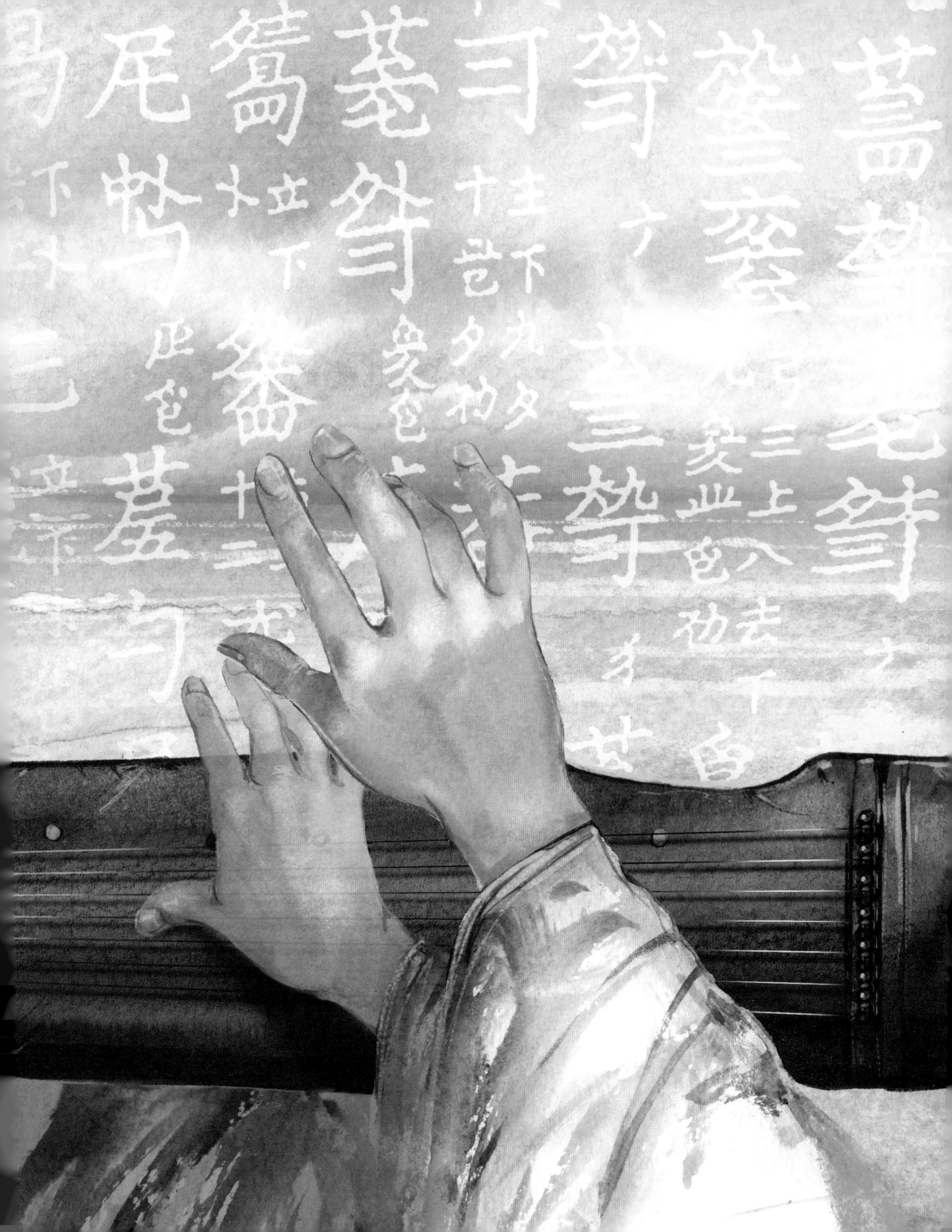

After listening to Boya's story, Ziqi sighed. "No wonder you became the best musician in China! You had the greatest teachers. The beautiful scenery and sounds of nature taught you everything you needed to know."

The two dear friends regretted that they had only just met. When Boya and Ziqi parted, they agreed to reunite on the Moon Festival the following year.

When the Moon Festival came the next year, Boya traveled to the Hanyang River as he had promised Ziqi. As the full moon rose in the sky, he began to play their favorite tune, "Lofty Mountains and Flowing Water."

The moon rose higher and higher, but Ziqi still did not appear. Finally, Boya asked a passerby about his friend. Unfortunately, Zhong Ziqi had been very ill and passed away a few days earlier. His last wish was that his tomb be built on the bank of the river. That way, Ziqi could hear Boya's music on the Moon Festival each year.

Upon hearing this, Boya felt like he had been struck by a thunderbolt. He sat at the foot of Ziqi's grave, playing their favorite melody. But this time, the music sounded sad and sorrowful.

After Boya finished, he broke all the strings on his guqin. Then he smashed the beloved instrument against the rocks, shattering it into many pieces. Brokenhearted, Boya cried out, "Since my dearest friend is gone, for whom can I play in the future?"

The story of Boya and Ziqi's friendship has been told for thousands of years. It illustrates the Chinese ideal of friendship. To honor them, a Guqin Terrace was built on the bank of Hanyang River, where they first met.

Today in China, a close friendship is called zhiyin. The word means "understanding the music." When two friends completely understand each other, they are like Boya and Ziqi, who understood music as if they shared one heart.